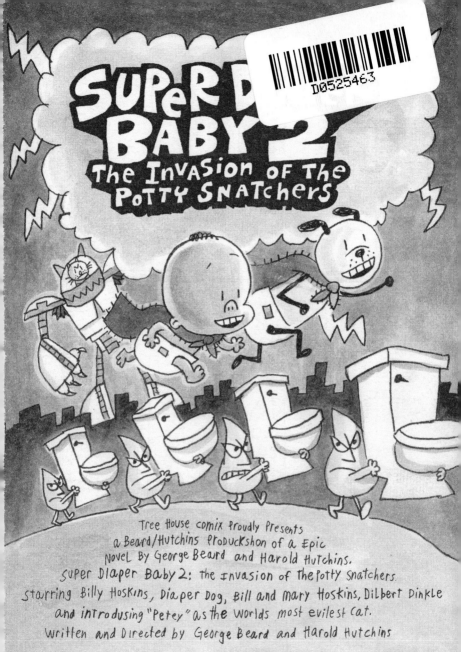

SUPER DIAPER BABY 2
THE INVASION OF THE POTTY SNATCHERS

Tree House comix Proudly Presents
a Beard/Hutchins Produckshon of a Epic
Novel By George Beard and Harold Hutchins.
Super Diaper Baby 2: the Invasion of the Potty Snatchers.
starring Billy Hoskins, Diaper Dog, Bill and Mary Hoskins, Dilbert Dinkle
and introdusing "Petey" as the Worlds most evilest Cat.
Written and Directed by George Beard and Harold Hutchins

■ SCHOLASTIC

this novel
has been
rated:

TA TotaLLy
AWesome!!!

some material may be too
Awesome for Boring old grown-ups

For Madison
Mancini

SCHOLASTIC CHILDREN'S BOOKS
AN IMPRINT OF SCHOLASTIC LTD
EUSTON HOUSE, 24 EVERSHOLT STREET
LONDON, NW1 1DB, UK
REGISTERED OFFICE: WESTFIELD ROAD, SOUTHAM, WARWICKSHIRE, CV47 0RA
SCHOLASTIC AND ASSOCIATED LOGOS ARE TRADEMARKS AND/OR
REGISTERED TRADEMARKS OF SCHOLASTIC INC.

FIRST PUBLISHED IN THE US BY SCHOLASTIC INC, 2011
FIRST PUBLISHED IN THE UK BY SCHOLASTIC LTD, 2011

TEXT AND ILLUSTRATION COPYRIGHT © DAV PILKEY, 2011
COVER ILLUSTRATION COPYRIGHT © DAV PILKEY, 2011

THE RIGHT OF DAV PILKEY TO BE IDENTIFIED AS THE AUTHOR
AND ILLUSTRATOR OF THIS WORK HAS BEEN ASSERTED BY HIM.

ISBN 978 1407 12998 3
ISBN (C&F) 978 1407 13009 5

A CIP CATALOGUE RECORD FOR THIS BOOK IS AVAILABLE FROM THE BRITISH LIBRARY.

PRINTED IN THE UK BY CPI BOOKMARQUE, CROYDON, SURREY.
PAPERS USED BY SCHOLASTIC CHILDREN'S BOOKS ARE MADE
FROM WOOD GROWN IN SUSTAINABLE FORESTS.

1 3 5 7 9 10 8 6 4 2

WWW.SCHOLASTIC.CO.UK/ZONE

The EPIC Story Behind the EPIC STORY of Super Diaper Baby

By George B and Harold H

Once upon a while ago, there were **2** RidonkULous Kids named George and Harold.

They dont get any awesomer than us!!!

me too!

They wrote a amazing Book called the "Adventures of super Diaper Baby."

BUT Unforchenetly, their mean PrincipeL, Mr Krupp read it.

It was the story of a baby who acksidentLy fell into some super power JUice.

Splash

He drank it and got super powers and stuff.

Also, a dog drank the Juice.

Glug
Glug

He became super powery, too!

The Baby and the dog are best friends now and they Live Together with their mum and dad.

They both wear diapers too!

BUT THEN ....

THIS IS GARBAGE!!!

Its the most off-ensive BOOK I ever read!!!

RIP

Why cant you Kids write about anything else besides POOP, huh?

scrach scrach

What else is there?

ZONG

Here! Read this Book!

FILE CABINET

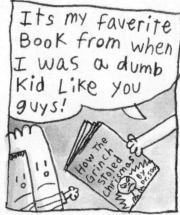

Its my faverite Book from when I was a dumb Kid Like you guys!

How the Grinch Stoled Chrismas BY Dr. Cool

Hey, how come the Last 7 pages are torn out?

Its more ReaLi-Stick that way!!!!

So George and Harold read the book and got inspired and stuff.

Hey This book is pretty good!

yeah!

HOW the Grinch STOLed CMAS

You know, I never thout Id say this, but maybe MR Krupp is right.

Maybe we **SHOULD** Think about other things to write About besides PooP.

Like what?

Hmmm... Hmmm...

scrach scrach

Scrach Scrach

How About Pee?

AWESOME!!!

So George and Harold starded creating their all-new epic Novel, Super Diaper Baby 2.

I bet Mr Krupp will be super happy!

Me too!

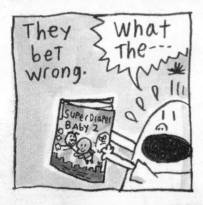

They bet wrong.

What The---

This is even more offensiver than your Last Book !!!

So thats the story of how Super Diaper Baby 2 was invented.

DETENSHON

as usual, we hope you Like it more Than Mr Krupp Did.

BIZZY WORK

BIZZY WORK

Chapters

12

One day the Hoskins family went to the park for a picnick.

This Looks Like a nice spot.

I will set up the Picnick while you boys play.

What would you Like to play, Billy?

me play airplane with Daddy.

15

WARNiNG

The following flip pages start out "cuteish", but get violentish (and even violentisher) as this novel goes along.

FLiPPER'S DiSGREShON ADViSED

FLiP·O·RAMA

HEres HOW it works!!!!

STEP 1
PLace your Left hand inside the dotted Lines marked "LEft Hand Here". HoLd The Book open FLAT.

STEP 2
GRasp the Right-hand Page with YOUR Right thumb and index finger (inside the dotted Lines marked "Right Thumb Here").

STEP 3
NOW QUICKLY FLip The Right-hand Page back and fourth UnTiL the Pitcher appears To Be Animated!

(for extra Fun, try adding your own sound Afecks).

17

FLIP-O-RAMA #1

(pages 19 and 21)

Remember, Flip <u>only</u> page 19. While you are Flipping, be shure you can see the pitcher on page 19 <u>And</u> the one on page 21.

IF you Flip Quickly, the two pitchers will start to look like <u>one</u> Animated pitcher.

Dont forget to add your own Sound Afecks!

Left Hand Here

Down Goes the Airplane...

Right
Thumb
Here

Up Goes the Airplane...

FLiP-O-RAMA 2

Remember --- FLip **OnLy** page 23. while you are flipping, be shure you can see the pitcher on page 23 **and** the one on page 25.

If you flip Quickly, The Two pitchers will start To Look Like one animated pitcher.

DonT forget Those sound afecks!

Left Hand Here

Down go the airplane

23

Right Thumb Here

up go the airplane

It's OK, Son. It was a acksident.

Now Lets enjoy this nice Lunch that mummy made.

BUT Then...

Hey Mister...

That big dumb bully Just stoled my doll. will you help me?

I shure will!

wait, Mr Hoskins...

28

29

So the Hoskinses started to eat thier picnick Lunch

BUT Then...

Hey mister...

Our ball got stuck up on the roof over there. Will you help us?

I shure will.

Wait--- my daddy got hurted!

Let super Diaper Baby handLe this!

30

31

Finally the Hos-kinses got BACK to finishing thier picnick Lunch.

Finally the Hos-kinses got BACK to finishing thier picnick Lunch.

BUT Then...

Hey mister!

My son broke his Big Toe playing Kickball. Can you drive us To The hospitel?

I shure will!!!

Wait, Mr Hoskins. That will Take Forever!!!

32

33

That night at the Hoskinses House...

Honey, whats wrong?

Oh nothing... It's just...

Its hard having Two Super Heros in the family.

Theyre Better than me at everything!!!

I feel so... "Ungood" at stuff.

34

I bet your still good at reading Bedtime storys!

Oh yeah!

I almost forgot. Im awesome at That!!!

Im going to go do that Right now!

Oh Billy?

BILLys Room

Knock KNOCK

Im am here to read you your faverite Bed-Time story!

Mecha-Frog and RoboToad are enemys

No daddy. Me read to you Tonite!

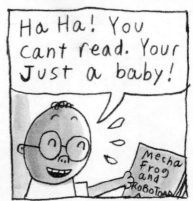

Ha Ha! You cant read. Your Just a baby!

Actually, he can read. The super power juice he drank also made him super smart!!! He Taught himself to read this morning!

AND SO...

..."no," shouted Mecha Frog. "not until you defeet my army of Ribbit Robots!"

This is Dr Dilbert Dinkle and his evil cat, Petey. Dr Dinkle is the one on the left with the beard and the male-pattern baldness. Petey is the one on the right with the stripes and the tail.

Remember that, now!

Tonight we will rob this Bank using my new invenchon: The Liquidater 2000!

Jim's BANK

it turns stuff into **WATER!!!**

It does this by rearanging molecules!

and then---

You have Bad Breath.

39

40

41

42

43

47

49

50

The city turned our water off and I'm thirsty!!!

That's a **YP**, Not a **MP!**

Well what am I suppost to Drink???

Listen, bub! I've been bizzy robbing banks all night! Quit Bugging me!

I'm going To sleep!

YAWN

AAAAAAh!

FLiP·O·RAMA 3

If you forgot how to do this already, please see your doctor. Afterwards, turn to page 17 for further instruckshons.

Left Hand Here.

Drinking Dr Dinkle

Right Thumb Here.

Drinking Dr Dinkle

58

CHAPTER 3
Daddy DiLema

Left Hand Here.

Snatcher Catchers

63

Right Thumb Here

Snatcher catchers

Left Hand
Here

Jacker smackers

Right
Thumb
Here

Jacker smackers

FLIP-O-RAMA 6

Left Hand Here

Cheater Beaters!

71

Right thumb Here

Cheater Beaters!

I cant believe it! I went to sleep and when I woke up, I got turned into pee!

Hey, I should call you "Rip van Tinkle!"

You better not!!!

alright, Rip van Tinkle. I wont.

YOUR in BIG TROUBLE!!!

Doncha mean "Urine" Big Trouble?

It's not funny!!! my whole body got turned into pee!!!

Hey! maybe you'll win a Peebody Award!!!

76

78

79

81

82

BUT I shall have my revenge, Petey! Oh yes, I shall have my revenge!!!!

I'm behind you **A HUNDREDTh of a PERSENT,** Rip Van Tinkle!

Would you CUT that out?!!? Its not very nise to call people names, you know!!!

BUT I'm one of the Bad Guys! I'm not suposed to be nise!!!

Oh yeah.

I forgot!

Tee-Hee! Being evil RULES!!!

84

CHAPTER 4 (PART 2)

HOW THE Pee STOLED POTTIES!

BY Dr George and Dr Harold

That Night Rip Van Tinkle
   was frowning a frown,
as he sneered at the houses
   below in the town.

No one knows why he was
   feeling so ruthless...
It could be because all his
   money was useless.

86

Or maybe because he was
    just feeling cranky.
Or possibly cuz his bad breath
    was so stanky.
But we think the very best
    reason might be
that he smelled like a bucket
    of twelve-day-old pee.

But whatever the reason
   his stank or his dough,
he stood up there hating
   the people below.
He snarled as he frowned
   feeling drearier and drearier.
"Those jerks in the city
Think Theyr'e so superier!

88

"They all be hatin'!
  But heres what I think:
I think things would change
  if they started to stink!

If all of those idiots
   smelled just like pee,
They wouldent be goin' Round
  disrespectin' me!!!"

And then RipVanTinkLe
Thought up a idea.
But we couldent Think up
a rhyme for "idea."

"I Know just what to do"
he started professin'.
"I'LL teach all of those good-
Smelling people a Lessen!"

So he took some scrap metal
and used an old wheel
To build a contrapshon
with Teeth made of steel.

He hammered its tail
and sharpened its claws,
and welded its wiskers
and titened its Jaws.

It took 24 hours
 From when he'd begun,
'Till the Robo-Kitty
 Three thousand was done.
"ALL I need is a driver.
 I need someone mean.
I need someone evil ♥
 to run my machine".

So he took his cat "Petey"
 and strapped him in tight...

...Then both of those villens
sneaked out in the night.

"Watch this," Rip Van Tinkle said
Laffing out Loud...
and soon he began to
turn into a cloud.

96

And when the pee cloud
was over the town,
the thunderclaps crashed
and the pee drops rained down.

Into the chimneys
the pee drops they flew
And they entered each house
knowing just what to do.

Each drop found
a wrench...

... and each
wrench found
a bolt...

...and soon
every Toilet
popped up
with a JoLt!

They carried each toilet
  Right out of each house, and
Into the jaws of the
  Kitty Three thousend.

Crunch! Crunch! went the robot
without too much trouble
and soon every potty
was crushed into rubbel!

But in one little house,
  on one little street,
One drip heard the sounds
  of two little feet.

The pee drop looked up
  and what did it see?
but a cute little tot
  with a fluffy blankie.

The baby looked down
and said, "MR Pee, Hey!
Why are you taking
our toilet away?"

And that mean little drip,
do you know what it did?
why, it made up a lie
and it said to the kid:

"Your toilet is broken---
  it squeaks when you flush it.
I'll take it away and I'll
  clean it and brush it.

I'll shine it right up
  -I'll fix it and oil it,
and soon I'll return with a
Good-as-new toilet."

And the baby believed what
the pee drop had said.
So it got him a juice box
and took him to bed.

BiLLyS
Room

And at Last when the baby
was sleeping and dreaming,
That nasty old pee drop
went on with its skeeming!

He carried The Toilet
Right out the door.
and once it was crushed,
He went back to get more.

The snatching of Potties
went on through the night,
And into the dawn of the
Mornings first Light.

109

And Once Every toiLet
was crushed by the cat,
The people awoke and cried,
"What up wit' dat?"

"Our toilets are gone!
Weve got to go Potty!
Oh, we do not Like this!
Oh, no we do notty!"

111

So they each crossed their legs
and squirmed all around,
And they squeezed and they clenched,
and they bobbed up and down.

'Till all of the people
were doing "Pee dances"
shouting, "Someone please help us,
or we'll wet our pantses!"

They wiggled all morning
   in torment and Trauma,
Just Like they're doing
   in this FLip-o-Rama →

Left Hand
Here

Pee-Dance
RevoLushon

Right
Thumb
Here

Pee-Dance
RevoLushon

Soon, warm liquid streams
with yellowish hues
flowed down their legs
and filled up their shoes.

And they sobbed as they stood
in their puddles of piddle,
But no one could help them.
Not even a little.

118

Chapter 5

the Aftermath

120

The pee drops formed a very large puddle...

...and out of that puddle came you-know-who!

Ha! Ha! Ha!

Ho! Ho! Ho!

He! He! He! He!

Everyone Everywhere smells Just Like Pee!

Now they all know what it's like to Be me!!!

Dude, were not doing the Rhyming thing Anymore.

Oh. Sorry.

121

So what's the next part of our evil plan?

next part?

Yeah, you know, what are we gonna do **Next**???

um... I don't know. wanna watch a movie or something?

That WASNT your **WHOLE PLAN**, was it?

What?

Are you saying we went through ALL that trouble Just so people would wet their pants and smell like pee?

umm... kinda.

AAAAUGH!

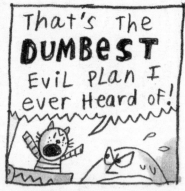

That's The **DUMBEST** EviL PLan I ever Heard of!

weLL if your so smart, why dont You think up a eviL PLan!!!

OK, I WiLL!!!

Hmmm... Let me think...

NoBody has a toiLet anymore...

Everybody has to go Pee-Pee...

I Got it!!!

124

BUT THEN

We interupt this show to tell you some important stuff!!!

5 Action News

As you all know, everybodys toilet got stoled last night.

5 Action news

Nobody has a plase to pee anymore so the mayor has drained the city's pool...

Please feel free to pee in this empty pool until our crisis is resolved!

Local kids had this to say:

This is Awesome!

I've been Peeing in that pool for years! Now I dont hAve to feel gilty!

me too!

in other news, a Giant Robotic cat is stealing all the citys diapers!

⑤ acTion news

Its going from store to store taking every diaper in town!!!

Diaper Depot

SALE

who will save us from this madness???!?

This Looks Like a job for us!

Hooray!

126

129

133

136

Left
Hand Here

Koo-Koo For Kitty Nip!

143

Koo-Koo For Kitty Nip!

POP

FLIP·O·
RAMA

Left Hand
Here

KiTTY FOR KOO-KOO Nip!

147

KITTY FOR KOO-KOO NIP!

SWISH!

He
Shoots!

He
scores!

CRASH

FUNNELS
"R" US

OPen
24 Hours

For all
your
Funnel Needs

LETS
TAKE
THIS
CAT
BURGLER
TO
JaiL

Oh Boy! JaiL!!

CHAPTER 6

The Revenge of
Rip Van Tinkle

153

154

157

158

160

FLIP-O-
RAMA

Left Hand
Here

Building Basher

Right
thumb
Here

Building Basher

Remember back a Long Time ago when me was really Little?

You mean Last week?

Yeah!

Well, remember when me put me's Juice Box in the freezer on acksident?

Heh-Heh! Yeah, it Froze Solid!

Hey!!! Your idea just gave me a idea!!!

Push down on the ground, Billy! Push as hard as you can!!!

167

Billy and Diaper Dog pushed and pushed...

...and slowly things began to move.

ALL we have to do now...

...is wrap this rope around him...

...and take him to a planet where he will never melt!

where?

why uranus of course!!!

BUT on the way, Billy got another good idea!

wisper wisper wisper

meanwhile at the Hoskinses House...

I'm am so worried about Billy and Diaper Dog!!! where could they be?

I don't Know sweat Heart.

BOOM

Hi mummy and Daddy!

BiLLY!

Daddy Theres a big Ice monster Outside!!!

I'm so glad your safe!!!

Daddy Look at the ice monster!!

OK, OK. LeTs Look at this silly ice monster of yours!

ILL Just open these curtins and take a peek!

183

Then Billy and Diaper Dog moved the Earth back to its proper place in space...

Left Hand Here.

say Cheese!!!

Right
thumb
Here

Say Cheese!!!

187

READ GEORGE AND HAROLD'S FIRST TWO EPIC ADVENTURES!

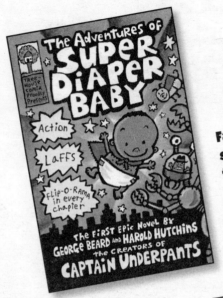

Faster than a speeding stroller, more powerful than diaper rash, and able to leap tall buildings without making poopy-stinkers, it's Super Diaper Baby!

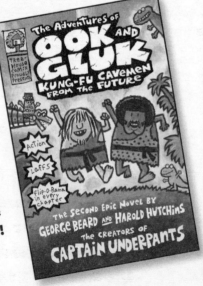

Meet Ook and Gluk, the two coolest caveboys to step out of the Stone Age!

COMING SOON

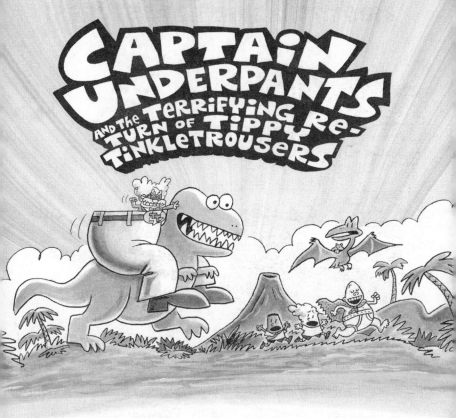

CAPTAIN UNDERPANTS AND THE TERRIFYING RE-TURN OF TIPPY TINKLETROUSERS

Whatever happened to Professor Poopypants, that tiny tornado of terror who traumatized the people of Piqua? He changed his name to Tippy Tinkletrousers, and he has a special surprise for anybody who thinks his NEW name is still funny. This looks like another job for the amazing Captain Underpants!